Rebecca of Sunnybrook Farm

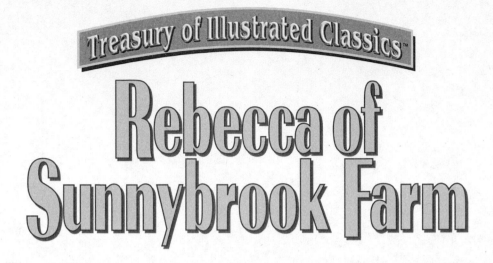

Treasury of Illustrated Classics™

Rebecca of Sunnybrook Farm

by
Kate Douglas Wiggin

Adapted by
Tracy Christopher

Illustrated by
Marchelene Manning

Modern Publishing
A Division of Unisystems, Inc.
New York, New York 10022

Series UPC: 39340

Cover art by Jael

Copyright ©2001, 2002 Kidsbooks, Inc.
230 Fifth Avenue
New York, New York 10001

This edition published by Modern Publishing,
a division of Unisystems, Inc.

Printed in Italy

Contents

Rebecca Rowena Randall

Mr. Jeremiah Cobb was hitching his horses to the stagecoach, thinking of the dusty road that lay between Maplewood and Riverboro, when a woman approached him.

"Is this the Riverboro stage?" she asked. When he nodded yes, the woman motioned to a young girl, who looked to be about eleven. "Could you take my daughter Rebecca to my sisters' house in Riverboro?" she asked. "Do you know

Miranda and Jane Sawyer? They live in a brick house in town."

"I know them well," Mr. Cobb replied. "I live just down the road from that fine brick house of theirs. My name is Jeremiah Cobb, and I'm pleased to meet you, ma'am."

"Thank you, Mr. Cobb. My name's Aurelia Randall, and my girl Rebecca is going to Riverboro to live with her aunts for a while. My sisters, the Sawyers, are expecting her. Tell them that Aurelia Randall sends her daughter and her love to both of them."

"I'll deliver both your girl and the message," Mr. Cobb said as he swung up to his seat on the driver's box.

"Will you please keep an eye on Rebecca during the journey, Mr. Cobb?" Mrs. Randall asked hesitantly. "You see, she's too talkative for her own good. If she can get out anywhere, or even get people to take the coach with her, she'll try to do it."

"Oh, Mother, don't worry," Rebecca chimed in. "It isn't as if I haven't traveled before, you know."

"As if going to Wareham and staying overnight constituted traveling," Mrs. Randall laughed, shaking her head and rolling her eyes upward at Mr. Cobb.

"It *did* count as traveling, Mother!" Rebecca insisted. "It was leaving the farm, and carrying lunch in a basket, and taking a ride on the train—and we carried our nightgowns!"

"No need to tell the whole village about our nightgowns," Rebecca's mother said sternly. "Now, try not to get into any mischief. Sit quietly in the coach, so you'll look nice and neat when you get to Miranda's. Don't be any trouble to Mr. Cobb," Mrs. Randall scolded as she carefully counted out Rebecca's coach fare into the driver's hand.

"I know, Mother, I know! I won't be any trouble. All I want to say is ..." Rebecca called out as Mr. Cobb urged

his horses into motion. "All I want to say is that it is indeed a journey when . . ." she insisted, her head out the coach window, "it is in fact a journey when you carry a nightgown!"

Mrs. Randall heaved a sigh as the word *nightgown* floated back, loud enough for all to hear. "Miranda and Jane will have their hands full with that young one," she said to herself as she climbed into her own wagon and turned the horses toward home, "but I hope they'll make something of my dear Rebecca."

The Road to Riverboro

Jeremiah Cobb had just settled back and was allowing his mind to drift to thoughts of home when he heard a small voice above the rattle and rumble of carriage wheels. When he looked down from his driver's box, he could see Rebecca hanging out of the window as far as safety would allow. She was trying to get his attention by waving a fancy pink parasol in his direction.

"Excuse me, Mr. Cobb," she cried as

he drew the horses to a halt. "Does it cost any more to ride up there on the box with you? It's so slippery and shiny down here that I rattle around on the seat until I'm black and blue. And the windows are so small that I can see only pieces of things."

Mr. Cobb waited until Rebecca's long speech ended, and then he boosted his talkative young passenger to a seat by his side on the box.

"Oh, this is ever so much better!" Rebecca exclaimed, adjusting her sun bonnet and pulling at her darned white cotton gloves. "This is like traveling! Down in the coach, I felt like our setting hen when we shut her up in the chicken coop. I am a real passenger now. I hope we have a long, long way to go!"

"Well, Riverboro's about two hours away from here," Mr. Cobb replied in an obliging tone of voice.

"Only two hours!" Rebecca sighed. "Then we will arrive at approximately half past one. The children at home on the farm will have had their dinner. My elder sister, Hannah, will have cleared all the dishes, and Mother will have gone to help cousin Ann. Have you ever heard of Randall's Farm?"

"It's not the old Hobbs place, is it?" Mr. Cobb searched his memory of the region, scratching his head.

"No, it's just Randall's Farm. At least that's what Mother calls it. I call it Sunnybrook Farm."

"I guess it doesn't make much of a difference what you might call it, as long as you know where it is," Mr. Cobb remarked.

Rebecca turned the full light of her eyes upon her driver in reproach, as she answered, "Oh, don't say that. You sound just like everyone else! It absolutely does make a difference what one calls things! When I say Randall's Farm, do you see what it looks like?"

"No, I can't say that I do," Mr. Cobb replied uneasily.

"But when I say Sunnybrook Farm, what do you think of?" Rebecca quizzed the old man.

Mr. Cobb felt like a fish removed from water and left gasping on the sand. Rebecca's eyes were searchlights that looked right through him in search of an imaginative answer. "I suppose there's a brook or stream somewhere nearby," hazarded Mr. Cobb—he simply was not a very imaginative person.

Rebecca looked disappointed but not quite disheartened with him. "That's not bad for a beginning," she said encouragingly. "There is a brook, but it is not just an ordinary stream. It has young trees and baby bushes on either side of it, for one thing. It's a shallow little chattering brook, with a white sandy bottom and lots of little shiny pebbles. Whenever there's a bit of sunshine to be had, the brook catches it, and, consequently, it's always full of sparkles, all day long.

"Are you hungry?" Rebecca continued, changing the subject. "I have some lunch, because Mother said that it would be a bad beginning to get to the brick house hungry and make Aunt Miranda give me something to eat first thing. It's a good day for growing crops and things, isn't it?"

"It is indeed," Mr. Cobb replied, amused by Rebecca's stream of chatter about so many different subjects at once. "It sure is hot today, though. Why don't you put up that pink parasol of yours to protect your head from the sun?"

"Oh, dear, no, I couldn't do that!" Rebecca protested in alarm. "I never put it up when the sun shines. It's too delicate. Pink fades awfully fast, you know. I only carry my parasol to church on cloudy Sundays. Sometimes the sun comes out all of a sudden, and I have a dreadful time trying to cover it up with my dress. My parasol is the dearest thing in life to me, but, oh, what a responsibility it is!"

It was beginning to dawn on Mr. Cobb that Rebecca was very different from most girls of her age. He took a second look at his young passenger—a look that she met with a childlike stare of friendly curiosity. The beige-colored calico of Rebecca's dress was faded, but very, very clean, and starched into stiff folds. From the little ruffle at the neck of the dress came a child's slender throat—long, brown, and thin. Rebecca's head seemed too small to bear the weight of the black braid that hung to her waist. She wore an odd little bonnet, trimmed with a twist of buff-colored ribbon and a cluster of black and orange porcupine quills that bristled over one ear, giving her the quaintest and most unusually striking appearance.

As to facial features, Rebecca's were not unusual, but she had the most extraordinary eyes. Under delicately

arched brows, they glowed like two stars, their dancing light half-hidden in lustrous brown darkness. Their gaze was brilliant and mysterious. The way she looked at you gave you the impression that she was looking directly past the obvious to something beyond. Rebecca's eyes were like faith—the substance of things hoped for, the evidence of things not seen.

Mr. Cobb found himself unable to find the words he wanted when describing Rebecca to his wife that evening. When discussing the remarkable passenger he had brought to Riverboro that day, he could only stammer in admiration that Rebecca had eyes that could knock a person galley-west.

Chapter 3

The Brick House

"**I** didn't volunteer to be the making of just any child," Miranda Sawyer said as she read her sister Aurelia's letter one last time before Rebecca's arrival. "I supposed, of course, that Aurelia would send us the one we asked for, but it's just like her to palm off that wild young one on us."

"Aurelia needs Hannah at home to help her with the other children," Jane Sawyer reminded Miranda. "We said originally that Rebecca or even Jenny

could come, in case Hannah was needed on the farm. Besides, Rebecca has had time to grow up and to mature."

"Or time to grow worse," Miranda mumbled irritably. "Moreover, if she makes as much work after her arrival as she has made this last week, we might as well give up hope of getting any rest ever again!"

"We've always kept a clean house, Rebecca or no Rebecca," Jane reminded her sister. "What I can't understand is why you've scrubbed and baked as you have all week for the arrival of this one child. You've practically bought everything up at Watson's dry-goods store—cleaned him out entirely," Jane teased her elder sister.

"I've seen Aurelia's house and her farm and so have you. I've seen that batch of seven children wearing one another's clothes and never caring whether they had them on right-side out or not. That child will arrive here without clothes fit to wear—she'll have brought Hannah's old shoes, John's undershirts, and Mark's socks, most likely. I suppose she's never had a thimble on her finger and hasn't the slightest notion of how to sew. She'll learn, though—I'll see to that. I've bought a piece of unbleached muslin and a piece of brown gingham for her to make her own dresses. I'm sure she won't pick up after herself, and she's probably never even seen a feather duster. She'll be as hard to train in our ways as if she were a heathen from another country!" Miranda concluded in a harsh tone.

Just then, both women heard the rumble of the stagecoach outside the house. Mr. Cobb was bringing Rebecca right to their front door!

"Miranda Sawyer, you've got a real lively girl here," Mr. Cobb said in greeting as he helped Rebecca down from the coach. "I guess she'll be a first-rate company keeper."

Miranda shuddered openly at the adjective *lively* being applied to a child—she believed firmly that children should be seen but not heard. "We're not much used to noise, Jane and I," she grumbled.

Mr. Cobb saw that he had said the wrong thing, but he was too unused to argument to explain himself. As he drove away, he tried to think of a safer word he might have used to describe his interesting young passenger.

"We'll take you up and show you your room, Rebecca," Miranda said. "Now, shut the mosquito-netting door tight behind you, to keep the flies out. It's not fly season yet, but I want you to start good habits right away here in the brick house. Take your bag along with you, so you won't have to make two trips. Always make your head save your heels. Wipe your feet on that braided rug. Put your parasol in the hall closet."

"Do you mind if I keep it in my room, please, Aunt Miranda?" Rebecca asked shyly. "It always seems safer to have it right here with me."

"There aren't any thieves hereabouts, and if there were, I'm certain that they wouldn't bother with taking your sunshade, but come along. Remember to always take the back stairs. We never use the front stairs because we don't want to get the carpet dirty. Your room is at the top of the stairs, here on the right. When you've washed your face and hands and brushed your hair, you can come back downstairs. "Say," Aunt Miranda said as she peered closely at her new charge, "haven't you got your dress on backwards?"

Rebecca drew her chin down and looked at the row of buttons running up and down the middle of her flat little chest. "Backwards? Oh, I see what you mean! With seven children back at the farm, Mother can't keep buttoning and

unbuttoning everyone all the time—we all have to dress ourselves. We're always buttoned up in front at Sunnybrook Farm. Mira's only three, but she's buttoned up in front, too."

Miranda said nothing, but the look she gave Jane fully expressed her disapproval of the way the children were being raised. What on earth would they do with an unruly child like Rebecca!

Sunday Thoughts

One week after Rebecca had settled into her aunts' brick house, she wrote a letter to her mother.

Dear Mother,
I am safely here in Riverboro. My dress did not get very rumpled and Aunt Jane helped me to iron it. I like the stagecoach driver, Mr. Cobb, very much—he said that he and Mrs. Cobb might take me to Milltown to see the fair someday.

The brick house looks just the same as you had described it. The parlor is splendid and gives you chills when you look in the door. However, we are never allowed to sit down in the parlor, because we might ruin something. The furniture is elegant, too, but there are no comfortable places to sit down, except in the kitchen. I think Aunt Miranda hates me. Hannah was the one she wanted, because Hannah's more obedient and doesn't answer back so quickly. I'm doing the best I can to get along and to obey her, though.

I like the school. Miss Dearborn can answer more questions than the teacher back home, but she still can't manage to answer all the questions I ask. She says I ask so many questions she can't keep up with me! I am smarter than all of the girls except one, but not so smart as two of the boys. My new friend Emma Jane Perkins can add and subtract in her head like a streak of lightning! She is in the third reader, but she does not like stories in books. I am in the sixth reader, but just because I cannot say the seven multiplication table, Miss Dearborn has threatened to put me in the baby primer class with Elijah and Elisha Simpson—little twins who don't come to school as often as they should during the winter because they don't have warm coats and shoes.

I spend afternoons after homework sewing brown gingham dresses. Emma Jane and the Simpson children get to play house or run on logs in the river, but their mothers don't know they're doing it. Their mothers are afraid they will drown. Aunt Miranda is afraid I'll get my clothes all wet and dirty, so she will not let me go out with the other children very often. I can play from half past five until suppertime, and after supper for a little while, and on Saturday afternoons after my chores.

People are saying that it's going to be a good year for apples and hay, so maybe you'll be able to pay a little more on the mortgage to the farm. Miss Dearborn asked the class what the object of education was, and I said that the object of mine was to help my mother pay off the mortgage. Unfortunately, Miss Dearborn repeated what I had said to Aunt Miranda, probably because she thought it was an amusing thing to say, but it certainly was a bad idea. Now I have to sew an extra dress as punishment, because Aunt

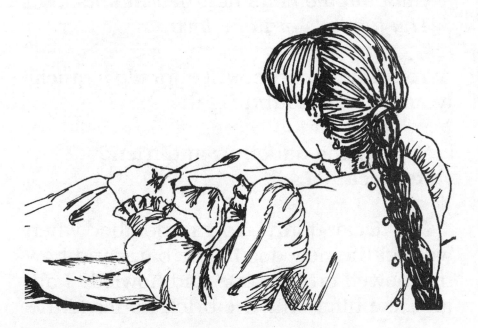

Miranda says that having a mortgage on a house is a disgrace and a blight to our family—rather like stealing or smallpox would be. She thinks that gossip will spread around Riverboro that the Sawyers have a sister who has mortgaged her farm.

I've written a poem for you about our mortgage:

Rise my soul, strain every nerve,
Thy mortgage to remove,
Gain thy mother's heartfelt thanks,
Thy family's grateful love.

You have to pronounce *family's* quickly, or it won't sound right.

Your loving daughter and friend,
Rebecca

P.S. Dear John—You remember when we tied the new dog in the barn and how he chewed on the rope and howled? I am just like him, only the brick house is the

barn and I cannot bite Aunt Miranda because I must be grateful. Education is going to be the making of me, so I can help you pay off Mother's mortgage when we both grow up. Tell Mark he can have my paint box, but I'd like him to keep from using all the red, in case I come home again. I hope that you and Hannah aren't getting tired of doing my chores in addition to your own.

Your loving sister and friend,

Rebecca

Chapter 5

A Pink Gingham Dress

Rebecca tried and tried to like her Aunt Miranda, but she just couldn't seem to do anything right in her aunt's eyes. Rebecca was a passionately human child, with no desire to be the angel of the house. But she did have a sense of duty and the desire to be good—respectably, decently good. Whenever she fell below this self-imposed standard, she was miserable. She did not like to be under her aunt's roof, eating food, wearing clothes, and studying from books provided by her aunt, yet not like Miranda most of the time. She felt that this was wrong and mean of her. Whenever the feeling of guilt became too strong within her, she made another desperate effort to please the grim and difficult women.

But how could Rebecca succeed when she was never quite herself in Aunt Miranda's presence? The hostile eyes, the sharp voice, the hard knotty fingers, the thin lips, the long silences—there was not a single feature of Rebecca's Aunt Miranda that appealed to her.

Rebecca was not the only child who was uncomfortable around Miranda. The Simpson twins were so afraid of her that they could not be persuaded to come to the door of the brick house to visit, even when Miss Jane held gingerbread cookies for them in her outstretched hands.

What sunshine in a shady place was

Aunt Jane to Rebecca! Aunt Jane, with her quiet voice, her understanding eyes, and her words of forgiveness and encouragement. She was such a help during those first difficult weeks, when Rebecca was trying to settle down to Miranda's rules. She did learn them, in part, but trying to mold herself to what seemed to her an extremely strict code of conduct made her feel much older than her years.

It is needless to say that Rebecca irritated her Aunt Miranda with every breath she drew. She continually started up the front stairs because it was the shortest route to her bedroom. She left the dipper on the shelf instead of hanging it over the water pail. She sat in the chair that the cat liked best. She did not close the screen door properly, letting flies into the house. She never stopped talking. She was always occupied with flowers, putting them in vases, pinning them on her dress, and sticking them in her hat.

Finally, and worst of all, Rebecca was the living reminder of her father, Lorenzo Randall. He had arrived in Riverboro twenty years before as a fancy-dance instructor, and managed to sweep young Aurelia Sawyer off her feet and out of her senses. The foolish Aurelia had married for romance and love. She had stayed with her impractical, romantic husband even when it was clear that he couldn't manage to make a success of any profession it occurred to him to try.

Aurelia's share of the modest Sawyer property had been invested in one thing after another by the handsome but luckless Lorenzo. He had managed to lose all of her money by the time he died of pneumonia during the winter Mira was born. His last investment had been a small, and more or less worthless, farm near Temperance, which now produced even less than was needed to pay the interest on the mortgage. To Miranda's disapproving mind, Rebecca looked exactly like Lorenzo—a black-haired beauty with eyes as big as cartwheels. She had also inherited his restless and overly intelligent spirit, along with a head full of romantic notions. Now she was living under Miranda's roof as a continual reminder of human impracticality and foolishness.

Miranda thought about these sad facts of human existence in the afternoons, when Rebecca took her sewing and sat beside Jane in the kitchen. To Rebecca, the pieces of brown gingham—destined to be the only material for her dresses—were endless. She made hard work of sewing, broke the thread, dropped her thimble, and pricked her fingers. She could not match the checks on the gingham, made crooked and puckered seams, and caused her needles to squeak endlessly as they poked their way along a hem. Fortunately, Aunt Jane had the

patience of a saint. Some small mea-
sure of skill was creeping into
Rebecca's fingers—fingers that held
pencil, paintbrush, and pen so cleverly
at school, but remained clumsy with
the dainty sewing needle at home.

When the second brown gingham
dress was completed, Rebecca seized
on what she thought would be an
excellent opportunity to ask her Aunt
Miranda if she could have another color
for the next dress.

"I bought a whole bolt of the brown," said Miranda in a matter-of-fact tone. "That will give you two more dresses, with plenty of material left over for new sleeves and patches as you grow taller. It will be more economical this way."

"I know," Rebecca replied, "but Mr. Watson said that he will take back part of the material and let us have some pink and blue for the same price."

"You mean to say that you've already asked him if you could do that?" Aunt Miranda asked crossly, shocked once again at her niece's boldness at negotiating with her elders.

"Yes, ma'am, I did," Rebecca answered.

"It was not your place to do that."

"I was helping Emma Jane choose aprons when I thought to ask him. I didn't think that you would mind that much which color gingham I had. I'll keep the pink as nice and clean as the brown—you'll see! Mr. Watson said that it will wash well, without fading,"

Rebecca reasoned.

"I am only too convinced that Mr. Watson is a splendid judge of washing," Aunt Miranda said sarcastically. "I simply do not approve of children being rigged out in fancy colors. Jane, what do you think?"

"I think it would be all right to let Rebecca have one pink and one blue

gingham," Jane replied gently, knowing that this was not the expected or desired answer to her elder sister's question. "A girl does get tired of sewing only one color. Besides, she'll look like a charity case if she is always wearing the same brown color with a white apron. The color brown doesn't suit her that well, either. She would look ever so much prettier in pink or blue!"

"Handsome is as handsome does," Aunt Miranda said drily. "There's no point in humoring that child about her looks. She is as vain as a peacock now—not that she has that much to be so vain about!"

"She's young and attracted to bright things!" Jane insisted. "I remember well enough how I felt at her age."

"You were young and extremely foolish at her age!"

"Yes, I was, and I thank my lucky stars for being that way. I only wish I could figure out how to bring back some of that foolishness into my old age, to brighten my declining years in this house!"

That speech managed to silence Aunt Miranda for a while. Aunt Jane won for Rebecca the pink gingham. Jane also showed her niece how to make a pretty trimming of narrow, white linen tape, by folding it in pointed shapes and sewing it down very flat with neat little stitches. Rebecca sewed and basted the trim with renewed energy and enthusiasm, in an effort to get the dress finished as quickly as possible. Miranda decided not to say any more about the matter, but she was not happy about being defeated in her attempts to remain head of her household.

Chapter 6

The Friday Recitation

Riverboro's schoolhouse stood on the crest of a hill, with rolling fields on one side, a stretch of woods on the other, and the river glinting in the distance. It had a flagpole on the side and two doors in front—one for boys and the other for girls. Not much besides the landscape was beautiful, however. All was bare and ugly and uncomfortable inside the school building. The villages along the river spent most of their tax money

maintaining bridges and roads, so they had little left for schools.

Miss Dearborn's desk and chair stood on a platform, near the pot-bellied stove. Other furnishings were limited to a map of the United States, two blackboards, and wooden desks with benches for the students, who only numbered twenty in Rebecca's time. The seats were higher in the back of the room—the older and longer-legged students sat there. They were greatly envied, because they were both nearer to the windows and farther from the teacher than the rest of the students.

One Friday each year was traditionally set aside for a public display of student progress. Rebecca had scarcely been at the school for a year when it was time for the next performance. Friday afternoon was always the time for the dialogues, songs, and recitations that made up the program of events. It cannot be said that the day was necessarily happy. Most of the children hated "speaking pieces," hated the burden

of learning them by heart, and dreaded forgetting their lines midway through their speech. Miss Dearborn commonly went home with a headache, and did not leave her bed during the rest of the afternoon or evening.

Very few parents attended these exercises. Those who did sat nervously on a bench in front of the schoolroom. Beads of cold sweat pearled on their foreheads as they listened to the all-too-familiar halts and stammers of their desperate children. Sometimes an extremely young child who had forgotten his or her poem would cast himself or herself, bellowing, on his or her mother's chest. The child would be taken outside, where he or she was sometimes kissed and occasionally scolded. In either case, the potential for failure always added an extra dash of gloom and dread to the occasion.

Rebecca's presence at school, however, had somehow produced a new burst of enthusiasm for this year's Friday recital.

She had taught Elijah and Elisha Simpson to recite a poem with such comical effect that they delighted themselves, the teacher, and the other children. Rebecca had composed for Susan, who lisped, a humorous poem in which Susan happily "impersonated" a lisping child. Rebecca had also volunteered to be Emma Jane's partner in a dialogue. Emma Jane was rather shy, but felt much more confident when supported by Rebecca's presence.

Miss Dearborn announced on Friday morning that the exercises promised to be so interesting that she had invited the doctor's wife, the minister's wife, two members of the school committee, and a few mothers to attend. She asked Huldah Meserve to decorate one of the blackboards and Rebecca to decorate the other. Huldah, who was the star artist of the school, chose to reproduce the map of North America. Rebecca preferred to draw things less realistically. Before the enchanted eyes of her classmates, there grew under her skillful fingers an American flag drawn in red, white, and blue chalk, with every star in its proper place, and every stripe fluttering in the breeze. Beside the flag appeared a figure of Columbia, copied from the top of a cigar box that held the crayons.

Miss Dearborn was very pleased. "I propose that we give Rebecca a big round of applause for such beautiful pictures—drawings of which the whole school may be proud!"

The children clapped heartily, and Dick Carter, leaping to his feet, waved his hat and gave a rousing cheer. Rebecca's heart leaped for joy, and to her confusion, she felt tears rising in her eyes. She could hardly see her way back to her seat. She had never before been singled out for applause. She had never been praised in this fashion, never crowned as in this wonderful, dazzling moment. Rebecca

took her seat in silence. Her heart was so full of grateful joy that she could hardly remember the words of her dialogue.

Miss Dearborn dismissed her students at close to noon, so that those who lived near enough could go home and change clothes. Emma Jane and Rebecca ran nearly every step of the way, bounding with excitement.

"Will your Aunt Miranda let you wear your best dress, or only your buff calico?" asked Emma Jane once they stopped to breathe at Rebecca's gate.

"I think I'll ask Aunt Jane," Rebecca replied. "Oh! If only my pink gingham were finished! I left Aunt Jane making the buttonholes this morning!"

"I'm going to ask my mother to let me wear her garnet ring," said Emma Jane. "It would look perfectly elegant flashing in the light when I point to your flag. Good-bye! Don't forget your lines! And don't wait for me to go back to school—I may get a ride."

Chapter 7

Show Time!

Rebecca tried the side door to the brick house, but she found it locked. Fortunately, she knew where her aunts kept the key. She retrieved the key from under the front step and unlocked the door. When she entered the dining room, she found her lunch laid out on the table with a note from Aunt Jane saying that she and Aunt Miranda had gone to a meeting with Mrs. Robinson, and that they would not be back before supper.

Rebecca swallowed a piece of bread and butter, and flew up the forbidden front steps to her bedroom. On the bed lay the pink gingham dress finished by Aunt Jane's kind hands. Could she wear it without asking permission first? Did the occasion justify a new costume? Or would her aunts think that she ought to save the new dress for the next Sunday school concert?

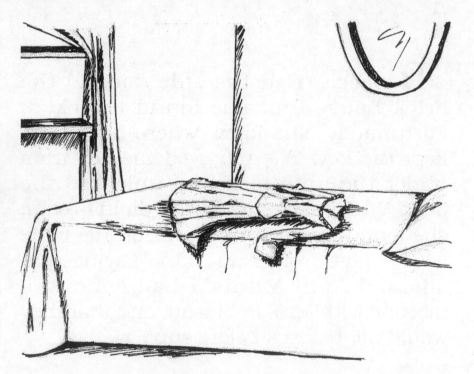

"I'll wear it," Rebecca said to herself. "My aunts aren't here to ask, and perhaps they won't mind. It's only gingham, after all, and the dress wouldn't be so terrific if it weren't new, and if it didn't have white tape trimming on it, and if it weren't pink." Rebecca slipped on the pretty new dress and managed to fasten all but the middle three buttons up the back—Emma Jane would have to help her with those. Then she changed her shoes and combed out her braids. She tied her wavy black hair into a single ponytail graced with a white ribbon.

Rebecca smiled at herself in the mirror. She felt ready to shine at her first recital. As she turned to leave her room, she spied her cherished pink sunshade. It was the perfect match for her dress, and her classmates had never seen it. It was too fancy for school, but she wouldn't take it into the schoolroom. She would wrap it in a piece of paper, just to show it, and then carry it coming back home.

Once Rebecca had finished wrapping her parasol, she glanced at the clock. Goodness! It was twenty minutes to one, and she would be late! She danced out the side door, pulled a pink rose from the bush at the gate, and covered the mile between the brick house and the school in an incredibly short time. She met Emma Jane, also breathless and magnificently dressed, at the entrance to the schoolhouse.

"Rebecca Rowena Randall!" exclaimed Emma Jane excitedly. "You're as handsome as a picture!"

"Nonsense!" laughed Rebecca. "It's the pink gingham."

"You're not so good-looking every day," insisted Emma Jane. "You're different somehow today. See my garnet ring? Mother scrubbed it in soap and water so it would shine! How on earth did you convince your Aunt Miranda to let you put on your brand-new dress?"

"She and Aunt Jane weren't home when I got there, so I didn't have a chance to ask," Rebecca answered, rather anxious all of a sudden. "Why do you ask? Do you think that they would have said no?"

"Miss Miranda always says no, doesn't she?" asked Emma Jane.

"Ye-es, that's true, but this afternoon is very special—almost like a Sunday school concert, don't you think?"

"Yes, it is, with your name on the

board, your flag behind us as we sing, and our elegant dialogue, and all that," Emma Jane reassured her friend.

The afternoon's performance was a succession of solid triumphs for everyone present. There were no failures, no tears, no parents ashamed of their offspring. Miss Dearborn's head did not ache. In fact, she heard many admiring remarks spoken about her teaching ability that afternoon.

Miss Dearborn wondered if this praise

belonged to her alone, or rather partly, at least, to Rebecca. The child had had no more to do than several of her classmates, but she had remained somehow in the forefront of events. The background positively refused to hold her, yet her worst enemy could not have called her pushy. She was simply ready and willing and never shy, without seeking chances for display. She

remained remarkably unaware of her own talents, and instead tried to bring others into whatever fun or entertainment there was to be had. Rebecca's clear soprano voice had soared above all the rest in the choruses, and everyone had taken note of her soulful singing and endless enthusiasm. Wherever she had stood had become the focal point of the performance.

Finally, the afternoon came to an end. It seemed to Rebecca as if she would never be so cool and calm again, as she walked slowly along the path, back toward the brick house. The certainty of having to do Saturday's chores and to help make jam the next day held no terrors for her. A certain radiant joy had flooded her soul.

There were thick black clouds gathering in the sky, but Rebecca took no note of them except to be glad that the sun had been covered up so that she could put up her sunshade. She felt as if she was walking at least a foot off the ground. Rebecca continued to feel extremely happy until she entered the side yard of the brick house and saw her Aunt Miranda standing with her hands on her hips in the open doorway. Then, when she realized that her aunt was really angry with her, Rebecca came back down to earth with a rush and a thudding heart.

Injustice at Home

"There you are, over an hour late. A little later and you'd have been caught in a thunderstorm, but you'd never notice," Aunt Miranda scolded Rebecca as soon as she caught sight of her entering the house. Then she turned to Aunt Jane, and continued the display of temper that she had begun before Rebecca's arrival. "If that's not bad enough, look at her rigged out in that new dress, stepping along with her father's dancing-school steps, and swinging that parasol for all the world as if she were play-acting on the stage. Now I'm the oldest, Jane, and I intend to have my say once and for all. If you don't like it, you can go into the kitchen until I've finished. Step right in here, Rebecca, I want to talk to you. What did you put on that new dress for, on a school day, without permission?"

"I had intended to ask you at lunchtime, but you weren't at home, so I couldn't," began Rebecca feebly.

"You did no such thing. You put it on because you were left alone, in spite of the fact that you knew well enough that I wouldn't have let you."

"If I'd been certain you wouldn't have let me, I'd never have done it," said Rebecca, trying to be truthful. "But I wasn't certain, and it was worth risking. I thought perhaps you might let me, if you knew that it was almost a real exhibition at school."

"Exhibition!" exclaimed Miranda. "You are certainly an exhibition enough by yourself. Were you also exhibiting your parasol?" she continued sarcastically.

"The parasol was silly," confessed Rebecca, hanging her head. "But it's been the only time in my whole life that I've had anything to match it, and it looked so beautiful with the pink dress! Emma Jane and I performed a dialogue about a city girl and a country girl. It occurred to me just as I was leaving the house that the parasol would be just the right thing for the city girl to hold. It did look nice! I haven't hurt my dress at all, Aunt Miranda."

"It's the underhandedness of your actions that's the worst," said Miranda coldly. "Let's talk about the other things that you've done today. You went up the front stairs to your room, when you know that walking up those steps dirties the carpet—I found your handkerchief halfway up. You never cleared away your lunch or did the dishes. Worst of all, you left the side door unlocked from lunchtime until we got home after three o'clock. Anybody could have come in here and stolen what they liked!"

Rebecca sat down heavily in her chair as Aunt Miranda listed her many sins. How could she have been so careless? The tears began to flow as she attempted to explain actions that were obviously too awful to justify or forgive.

"Oh, I'm so sorry!" Rebecca wailed. "I was decorating the schoolroom, and I left late and had to run all the way home. It was hard getting into my dress alone, and I hadn't time to eat but a mouthful of bread. Just at the last minute, when I honestly—honestly—would have remembered to clear the table and wash the dishes, I looked at the clock. I knew I would have to run all the way back to school to be in time to form the line! I thought how dreadful it would be to arrive late and get my first black mark on a Friday afternoon, with the minister's wife and the doctor's wife and the school committee all there. I was in such a rush that I simply flew out the door and forgot to lock it!"

"All right, there's no need to get hysterical," Aunt Miranda said sternly. "There's no use crying over spilt milk. An ounce of good behavior would be worth a pound of sorrys and repentance, especially in your case. Take that rose out of your dress and let me look at the spot it has made on your collar and the rusty holes where the wet pin went in. It looks all right, but it's more by luck than by planning on your part. I've got no patience with your flowers and flowing locks and all your airs and graces— you put on airs just like that ne'er-do-well father of yours used to do."

Rebecca lifted her head in a flash. Her mother had told her that she must always stand up for her father, because nothing had ever gone his way in life. He would not have died so young and so broke if he hadn't had such bad luck.

"Look here, Aunt Miranda," Rebecca said fiercely, "I'll be as good as I know how to be. I'll obey you as well as I know how. I'll never leave the door unlocked again, but I won't have my father called names. He was a p-perfectly l-lovely father. That's what he was, and it's mean to call him names."

"Don't you dare answer me back in

that impertinent way, Rebecca! Your father was a vain, foolish, lazy man! You may as well hear it from me before you hear it from the whole town. He spent your mother's money, and he left her with seven children to provide for."

"It's s-something to leave s-seven nice children," sobbed Rebecca.

"Not when your mother has to work her fingers to the bone on that farm, just to keep the bank from taking it back. Not when other folks like your Aunt Jane and I have to help feed, clothe, and educate those seven children," Miranda said pointedly. "Now, you go upstairs and go to bed. I want you to stay in your room until morning. You'll find a bowl of crackers and milk on your dresser for dinner. I don't want to hear another sound from you until breakfast time. Jane, run and take the dish towels off the line. We're going to have a terrible storm."

"We've had it already, I think," Jane

answered quietly. "I don't often speak my mind, Miranda," she continued once she was certain that Rebecca was out of earshot, "but you ought not to have said what you did about Lorenzo Randall. He was what he was, but he was Rebecca's father. Aurelia always said that he was a good husband to her."

"Yes, but the truth needs telling, every now and then. As far as I'm concerned, that child will never amount to anything until she gets rid of what she inherited from her father, namely his imagination and his impractical, romantic notions about life. I'm glad I said just what I did."

"I dare say you are," remarked Jane, with what might be described as one of her annual bursts of courage. "But all the same, Miranda, it wasn't good manners. It wasn't very charitable or loving of you, either."

Chapter 9

The Would-be Runaway

Rebecca closed the door to her room wearily. She took off the beloved pink gingham dress with trembling fingers. She smoothed it out carefully, pinched up the white ruffle at the front, and laid it away in her drawer with a little sob at the idea of the roughness of life. The withered pink rose she had been holding fell to the floor. Rebecca thought to herself, "Just like my happy day!"

Nothing showed quite so clearly the

intelligent child she was than the fact that she instantly recognized the symbolism of the rose. She laid it in the drawer with her dress, as if she were burying the whole episode with all of its sad memories. It was a child's poetic instinct with a dawning hint of womanly feeling in it.

Rebecca combed her hair. All the while, the resolve grew in her mind that she would leave the brick house and go back to her beloved Sunnybrook Farm. She would not be taken back with open arms—there were too many children for that—but she would help her mother with the house and send Hannah to

Riverboro in her place. "I hope she'll like it better than I have," Rebecca thought in a momentary burst of temper.

Rebecca sat down by the window and watched the rain streaming down. She had hoped that Aunt Miranda would be pleased that her niece had succeeded so well at school, but there seemed no hope of pleasing her—in that respect or in any other. Rebecca would just have to go

back to Maplewood on the stage the next day with Mr. Cobb, and then get cousin Ann to take her back to the farm. She would slip away without telling her aunts that she was leaving. They would find her gone before breakfast.

Rebecca never stopped very long to think through a plan. Once she had decided to run away, she put on her oldest clothes and shoes. Then she wrapped her nightgown, comb, and toothbrush in a pillowcase, and dropped the small bundle softly out of her bedroom window. She scrambled out of the window after it, then flew up the road in the rainstorm.

Jeremiah Cobb was sitting at his kitchen table when he caught sight of Rebecca at his back door. Rebecca's face was so swollen with tears and so full of misery that for a moment he scarcely recognized her. His big heart went out to her in her trouble. He wanted her to be the first to tell him of it, so he decided that he would pretend that he hadn't noticed anything was wrong.

"Well, I never! It's my little lady passenger! Come to call on us, have you? You come right in and dry yourself by the stove. Mrs. Cobb has gone to nurse old Seth Strout through a bad case of the flu, but you'll stay and have a cup of tea with me, won't you?" he coaxed.

"Oh, Mr. Cobb, I've run away from the brick house, and I want to go back to the farm!" Rebecca cried. "Will you and Mrs. Cobb let me stay here tonight and take me up to Maplewood in the stage in the morning? I haven't got any money for my fare, but I'll earn it somehow afterwards and I'll send it to you."

"Well, we certainly won't argue over money, you and I. But I'd like to hear why you've decided to leave us before we've even had the opportunity to go to the fair together at Milltown. Why don't you tell me what has happened?"

Rebecca recounted the history of her trouble. Tragic as that history seemed to her passionate mind, she told it truthfully and without exaggeration. Mr. Cobb did not interrupt. He listened carefully to her tale, and tried to think of a way to resolve this terrible situation for the good of all concerned.

Chapter 10

A Tricky Return

"**Y**ou *will* take me to Maplewood, won't you, Mr. Cobb?" Rebecca pleaded as she ended her narrative.

"Don't you fret," he answered, planning his replies carefully. "I'll see the lady passenger through her trouble somehow. Now, sit down and have a bite of something to eat. Spread some of that good jam Mrs. Cobb makes on that piece of bread. Would you be so kind as to pour me another cup of tea?"

Comforted by the old man's tone, Rebecca began to enjoy the dignity of sitting in Mrs. Cobb's seat. She smoothed her hair, dried her eyes, and poured tea for both of them from the blue china teapot.

"I suppose your mother will be awfully glad to see you back home again," Mr. Cobb began.

"She won't like it that I ran away, and she'll be sorry that I couldn't succeed at pleasing Aunt Miranda. But I'll make her understand," Rebecca explained.

"I suppose she was thinking of your education by sending you here in the first place." Mr. Cobb pointed out. "But you can go to school back in Temperance."

"They have school only two months of the year in Temperance, but the farm's too far away from all the other schools," Rebecca replied. She was a little less sure of her plans all of a sudden.

"Oh, well, there are other things in this world besides education," Mr. Cobb continued, attacking a piece of apple pie.

"Ye-es, though Mother thought that education would be the making of me," Rebecca said sadly, choking back a sob as she tried to drink her tea.

"It will be nice for you to be all together again on the farm—such a house full of children!"

"It's too full—that's the trouble. I'll make my sister Hannah come to Riverboro in my place."

"What if Miranda and Jane don't want any more of you to come? Your aunts will be kind of mad at you for running away, you know. You can't really blame them for being upset about that," Mr. Cobb argued.

This was quite a new thought—that the brick house might be closed to Hannah, once her sister Rebecca had turned her back upon its cold hospitality.

"No use talking about it, anymore." Mr. Cobb shrugged, then pursued another strategy. "How's the school down here in Riverboro—pretty good?"

"Oh, it's a splendid school! Miss Dearborn is a wonderful teacher!" Rebecca exclaimed excitedly.

"You like her, do you? Well, she

certainly returns your feelings. Mrs. Cobb was down at the store this afternoon. She met Miss Dearborn on the bridge on her way back home. They got to talking about school. 'How is the little girl from Temperance doing?' my wife asks. 'Oh, she's the best scholar I have!' says Miss Dearborn. 'I could teach school from sunrise to sunset if all my scholars were as bright and as willing as Rebecca Randall.'"

"She said that?" glowed Rebecca, her smile dimpling in an instant. "I'll study the covers right off the books after this!"

"You mean, you would study that hard if you had decided to stay here in Riverboro," Mr. Cobb reminded her. "But you've decided to give it up because you're so angry with that Miranda Sawyer. Not that I blame you for being mad. She's cranky and she's sour, like she's been eating green apples all her life. She is difficult, and you're not a very patient person, I guess."

"No, I guess I'm not a very patient person," Rebecca admitted.

"Well, you're not wrong to lose patience with your aunt. She's terribly hard to please. Plus, she kind of heaves benefits at your head as if they were bricks. Although, she does give you new clothes, and a good place to live, and a fine education. Those are all benefits that you may eventually help repay with your good behavior.

"Is your Aunt Jane any easier to get along with?" Mr. Cobb asked, changing his tactics yet again.

"Oh, Aunt Jane and I get along splendidly," said Rebecca. "She's just as good and as kind as she can be. I like her better all the time. I'd let her scold me all day long, for I feel that she understands me."

"Your Aunt Jane will probably be very sorry tomorrow morning when she finds out that you've gone away. But, never mind, it can't be helped. She no doubt enjoys your company a great deal. In fact, Mrs. Cobb told me the other day that she had seen your Aunt Jane in town. 'You wouldn't know the brick house,' Jane said to her. 'I'm keeping a sewing school, and my student has sewn three beautiful dresses, the latest in pink gingham. I'm even thinking of reliving my youth by going to the church picnic with Rebecca!' According to my wife, it seemed pretty clear that Jane Sawyer had never looked so young or so happy."

Mr. Cobb knew that those final words had hit home. There was a silence that could be felt in the little kitchen, a silence made louder by the fact that the rain had stopped outside. A rainbow had appeared, visible from the kitchen window in the early evening light. Mr. Cobb seemed to have built another rainbow over Rebecca's troubles, one that would lead her happily back to the brick house.

"The storm's over," Mr. Cobb said with a wink and a smile. "It has cleared the air and washed the face of the earth nice and clean. Tomorrow, everything will shine like a new pin."

"Yes, tomorrow will mean a new day and a fresh start. I'm going to stay here and—and catch some bricks if I have to. I'm going to catch them without throwing them back, either," Rebecca said, grinning.

Mr. Cobb drove her back home and helped her sneak back through the window of her bedroom. Her aunts were never made aware that she had planned to run away. When Rebecca found herself back in her own bed that night, she felt a kind of peace stealing over her. She had been saved from foolishness and error. She had been kept from troubling her poor mother and embarrassing her aunts. Her heart was melted now. She felt determined to win her Aunt Miranda's approval.

It would have been some comfort to Rebecca if she had known that Miranda Sawyer had passed an equally uncomfortable night. She regretted her words and her harshness to the point where she made a promise to try to be less severe with her niece in the future.

Chapter 11

The Banquet Lamp

Just before the Thanksgiving of Rebecca's fourteenth year, the affairs of her friends, the Simpsons, reached what might have been called a crisis, even in their family. The Simpsons had long suffered from poverty and uncertainty. Mr. Simpson had spent his whole life taking things from neighbors without asking and with no intention of returning them. He considered what he did "borrowing"—taking items that were not in active use from his neighbors' barns and fields.

Mr. Simpson's neighbors didn't see his behavior in the same way that he did, however. They called it stealing. Mr. Simpson had been caught and sent to jail recently for stealing, and this left his family even worse off than ever. There was little to eat and less to wear,

although Mrs. Simpson did, as always, her very best to provide for her children.

In the chill of a gloomy early September, with the vision of other people's plump turkeys, corn, squash, and pumpkins being gathered into barns, the young Simpsons looked for some inexpensive form of excitement. They settled upon the idea of selling soap for prizes. They sold enough to their neighbors during the months of September and October to win a children's wagon. This wagon was not well made, but they had fun giving one another rides over bumpy country roads.

In November, the Simpson children set their sights on a more ambitious prize: a banquet lamp, which looked to be about eight feet tall in the catalogue of prizes issued by the soap company. It was made of polished brass, but often mistaken for solid gold, according to the description in the catalogue. The shade

that accompanied it as a prize for selling an extra hundred bars of soap was of crinkled crepe paper in "a dozen top-choice decorator colors".

Seesaw Simpson, a boy of fourteen who scoffed at the idea of selling soap, was not part of the sales team. Clara Belle Simpson was a fairly successful door-to-door salesperson, but Susan, who lisped and could only say "thoap", never sold a bar. The twins, who were too young to be trusted thoroughly, were given only six bars at a time. They were sent on their rounds with a document stating the price per bar, per dozen, and per box of one hundred bars.

Rebecca and her friend Emma Jane offered to help on a day when they were going to travel three or four miles by wagon to see Emma Jane's cousins in North Riverboro. They wanted to see what they could do in the way of stirring up popular demand for the Snow-White and Rose-Red brand—the former a laundry soap and the latter intended for use in the bath.

Rebecca and Emma Jane had a lot of fun preparing their sales pitch in Emma Jane's attic. They had the soap company's standard speech to memorize. They also remembered the dramatic delivery of a similar speech given by a patent-medicine salesman when he was working at the Milltown Fair. His method of persuasion, once observed, could never be forgotten. Rebecca practiced it on Emma Jane, and then they reversed roles.

"Can I sell you a little soap this afternoon? It is called the Snow-White and Rose-Red brand, twelve bars in a decorative box, only twenty cents for the white and twenty-five for the red. This soap is made from the purest ingredients. The ingredients are so pure that they could indeed be eaten by any invalid without doing the slightest harm," Rebecca began.

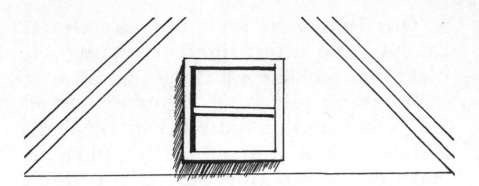

"Oh, Rebecca, let's not say that!" Emma Jane interrupted, laughing. "It makes me feel like a fool."

"It doesn't take a lot to make you feel like a fool, Emma Jane Perkins. I don't feel like a fool quite so easily. All right, leave out the eating part if you don't like it. But don't blame me if you can't sell as much soap as I do. Now you go on," Rebecca insisted.

"The Snow-White brand is probably the most remarkable laundry soap ever manufactured," Emma Jane continued. "Soak your clothes in water, rubbing all spots lightly with the soap. Leave them overnight, and in the morning the youngest baby could wash them clean without the slightest effort."

"Babe, not baby," corrected Rebecca, looking at the brochure.

"It's the exact same thing," argued Emma Jane.

"Of course it's the same thing, but a baby has got to be called a babe or infant in our sales pitch. It has to sound the same way it would in poetry. Would you rather use the word infant?"

"No," grumbled Emma Jane, "infant is even worse than babe. Rebecca, don't you think it would be a good idea to experiment with what it claims in this part about babes washing laundry? We could have Elijah and Elisha try out the soap before we begin advertising it in this way."

"I can't imagine a baby doing the laundry with any brand of soap," answered Rebecca. "It must be possible, or they would never dare print such a thing. Let's just take the soap company's claims on faith. Oh, won't we have fun, Emma Jane? At some of the houses where they don't know me at all, I won't be a bit nervous. I shall give the whole speech—invalid, babe, and all! Perhaps I shall even say the last sentence, if I can remember it: 'We sound every chord in the great macrocosm of satisfaction.' Isn't that grand?"

Chapter 12

Snow-White and Rose-Red

Emma Jane and Rebecca prepared and practiced their soap-selling speech all of Friday afternoon and evening. Saturday was the big sales event. The pair would have the old white horse, so that they could drive themselves to North Riverboro, eat lunch with Emma Jane's cousins, and return at four o'clock on the dot.

When the girls asked Mrs. Perkins if they could stop at just a few houses on their way to and from North Riverboro to sell a few bars of soap, Mrs. Perkins was not so sure that this was a good idea. She did not mind her daughter amusing herself in this way, but she was nervous about letting the niece of the difficult Miranda Sawyer do such a thing. However, the girls persuaded her that they were doing it to help the Simpsons get a banquet lamp by Christmas, and Mrs. Perkins finally agreed.

The girls stopped by Mr. Watson's dry-goods store, and arranged for three hundred-bar boxes of soap to be charged to Clara Belle Simpson's account. These were lifted onto the back of the wagon. A happier pair never drove out along the country road leading to North Riverboro. It was a glorious Indian summer day. There were still many leaves on the oaks and maples, making a good show of autumn color for early November. The air was like sparkling cider. Every field had heaps of squash and potatoes ready for the barn and the market. Rebecca stood up in the wagon and recited a poem that she had composed for the glory of the day:

"Great, wide, beautiful, wonderful World,
With the wonderful water 'round you
   curled,
The wonderful grass upon your breast,
World, you are beautifully dressed!"

The beauty of the day was not necessarily enough for success at selling soap, however. After an hour's worth of taking turns holding the horse and approaching potential customers, Emma Jane had only managed to sell three individual bars. Rebecca had sold three small boxes of a dozen bars each. Housewives looked at Emma Jane and desired no soap. They listened to her description of its merits and advantages, and still desired none. Rebecca's innate spark and gift of speech made her a more effective salesperson. The people with whom she conversed either remembered their current need of soap, or reminded themselves that they would need some at some point in the future. But neither girl had sold enough, and both were growing rather tired and disheartened in the face of rejection.

"It's your turn, Rebecca, and I'm glad, too," said Emma Jane wearily. "I'm not sure who lives here. It doesn't look like anyone is at home right now. If no one answers, you'll have to take the next house, too. It will still be your turn—I'm really tired!"

Rebecca went up the driveway to the side door of a big farmhouse, where there was a large porch. Seated in a rocking chair was a good-looking man. Rebecca couldn't tell if he was young or middle-aged. He had an air of the city about him. He had a well-shaven face, well-trimmed mustache, and nicely tailored clothes. Rebecca found herself a little shy at the idea of asking such a man if he needed soap. But it was too late to do anything else except explain what she was doing standing in the middle of his driveway.

"Excuse me, sir," she began. "Is the lady of the house at home?"

"I am the lady of the house, at the present moment," said the stranger with an amused smile. "What can I do for you?"

"Have you ever heard of the—would

you like, I mean—do you need any soap?" Rebecca asked haltingly.

"Do I look as if I need soap?" he joked.

Rebecca smiled, her dimples flashing. "I didn't mean that. I have some soap to sell. I mean, I would like to introduce to you a very remarkable soap, the best now on the market. It's called the—"

Rebecca continued, suddenly remembering her sales pitch in full.

"Oh! Wait a minute!" the gentleman interrupted. "I think I know the soap to which you refer. Made out of the purest vegetable fat, isn't it?"

"The very purest," echoed Rebecca.

"And a child could do the Monday washing with it and use no force to scrub out the dirt."

"A babe," corrected Rebecca.

"Oh! A babe, is it, now? That child grows younger every year!"

This was good luck, indeed, to find a customer who knew all the qualities and merits of this particular brand of soap.

Rebecca accepted an invitation to sit down on a stool near the edge of the porch. She pointed out all the decorative features of the box that held a dozen bars of the Rose-Red soap. She gave her prices per bar, per box, and per case of both the Rose-Red and the Snow-White varieties. The conversation soon went from soap to other topics. Soon Rebecca forgot all about Emma Jane waiting at the gate. She chattered away as if she had known this grand gentleman in the rocking chair all her life.

The Soap Sale
of the Century

"I'm keeping house today, but I don't live here," explained the delightful gentleman, as he and Rebecca continued their conversation on the porch. "I'm just on an extended vacation with my aunt, who has gone to Portland to visit some relatives. I used to live in this region as a boy. I am very fond of this part of the world."

"I don't think anything takes the place of the farm where one lived when one was a child," observed Rebecca in her fanciest English.

"So, you consider your childhood a thing of the past, do you, young lady?"

"I can still remember it," answered Rebecca seriously, "though it seems a long time ago."

"I can certainly remember mine. A particularly unpleasant one it was, too!" said the stranger.

"So was mine," sighed Rebecca. "What was your worst trouble?"

"Lack of food and clothes, for the most part," he answered.

"Oh!" exclaimed Rebecca in sympathy. "Mine was no shoes and too many brothers and sisters and not enough books. But you're all right and much happier now, aren't you?" she asked. He looked handsome and well-fed and wealthy. Yet anyone who looked closely could see that his eyes were tired and his mouth drooped sadly whenever he was not speaking.

"I'm doing pretty well, now. Thank you very much for inquiring," said the man with a broad smile. "Now, tell me, how much soap do you think I should buy from you today?"

"How much does your aunt have in storage now?" suggested the experienced sales agent. "And how much does she generally use?"

"Oh, I haven't the slightest idea, but soap keeps for a long time, doesn't it?"

"I'm not certain, but I have the brochure right here in my pocket. I can look it up for you," Rebecca answered

truthfully, as she drew the document from her dress pocket.

"What are you going to do with the magnificent profits you get from this business?" Rebecca's customer asked.

"We are not selling for our own benefit," Rebecca confided. "My friend Emma Jane, who is holding the horse at the gate, is the daughter of a very rich blacksmith. She doesn't need any money. I am poor, but I live with my aunts in a brick house in town. They would not like to think of me as a door-to-door peddler. Emma Jane and I are only trying to help our friends, the Simpsons, win a prize. They are not nearly as well off as we are."

Rebecca had never thought of mentioning the circumstances of the Simpsons to her previous customers, but this gentleman had such patience and seemed to want to hear all about them. So she found herself describing the bad borrowing habits of Mr. Simpson, and the hardships endured by the Simpson family as a whole—their joyless life, their poverty, and their need of a banquet lamp with a crepe paper shade to brighten their existence.

"I have no doubt that the Simpsons would find this lamp useful," said the gentleman. "They should have it if they want it, especially since you and your friend are working so hard to help them get it. I've known what it was myself to do without a banquet lamp. Now, give me the order form, and let's do some calculations. How much do the Simpsons lack at this moment?"

"If they sell two hundred more bars total for this month and the next, they can have the lamp by Christmas," Rebecca answered. "With a hundred more, they can get the shade for it by next summer. But I'm afraid that I won't be able to sell much after today, because my Aunt Miranda may disapprove. Today she wasn't home to ask. Mrs. Perkins, Emma Jane's mother, said that she supposed it would be all right, just for today."

"I see. Well, here's what we'll do. I will take three hundred bars today, and that will cover everything—lamp, shade, and all."

Rebecca's stool was dangerously near the edge of the porch. As she heard this fantastic proposal, she made a sudden movement, tipped over, and disappeared head first into a clump of lilac bushes. It was a very

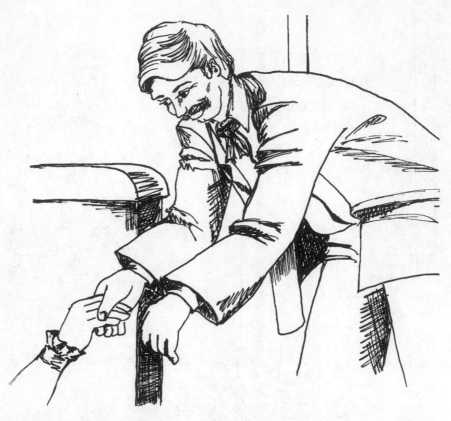

short distance to fall, fortunately. The amused philanthropist helped her up and set her on her feet again.

"You should never seem surprised when you have taken such a large order," he teased her with a smile. "You ought to have replied, 'Can't you make it three hundred and fifty bars?'

instead of falling off the porch in that unbusinesslike manner."

"I could never say anything so bold!" Rebecca exclaimed, blushing scarlet. "But it doesn't seem right for you to buy so much soap. Are you sure that you can afford it all?"

"If I can't, I'll save on something else."

"What if your aunt doesn't like this brand of soap?"

"My aunt always likes what I like."

"Mine *never* likes what I like!" Rebecca couldn't help exclaiming.

"Then there's something wrong with your aunt!" the man replied.

"Or with me," said Rebecca, laughing.

"May I ask the name of my excellent and persuasive saleslady, so that I may remember it a decade later, when I'll no doubt need more soap?"

"Rebecca Rowena Randall, sir."

"What? All three? Your mother was generous with names. Would you like to know the name of your best customer to date?"

"I think I know already! I'm sure you must be Mr. Aladdin of the Arabian Nights. Mr. Aladdin of the magic lamp!"

"Well, you're not too far wrong. My name is Mr. Adam Ladd, at your service. Why don't we go tell Emma Jane that you two have sold out your supply of soap in one fell swoop?" he suggested.

Together they went back down the driveway, where Mr. Ladd lifted out the remaining cases of soap and then helped the two girls back onto the driver's seat of the wagon. They all agreed to arrange for the lamp to arrive as a surprise for the Simpsons on Thanksgiving Day. Then the two girls went on their way. As they left, they broke into another chorus of thanks and of good-byes, during which tears of joy welled up in Rebecca's eyes.

"Oh, don't mention it!" Mr. Ladd called out as the white horse pulled into the road. "I was a sort of traveling salesman myself at one point, years ago. I like to see the thing well done. Good-bye, Miss

Rebecca Rowena! Just let me know whenever you have anything else to sell, for I am certain beforehand that I shall want the item in question!"

On Thanksgiving Day, the banquet lamp arrived in a large packing box. It was taken out and set up by Seesaw Simpson, who suddenly began to admire and respect the business ability of his sisters and friends. Rebecca could see,

from her own window in the brick house, the gorgeous trophy lit up and shining from the Simpsons' living-room window. All winter long, the banquet lamp sent a blaze of crimson glory through its red paper shade out into the darkness of snowy nights.

Chapter 14

High School at Wareham

Rebecca's fifteenth birthday had come and gone. She had outgrown the one-room schoolhouse in Riverboro, and had been sent to the senior high school in Wareham. Rebecca's intention was to complete the three-year course of study in two years, since her mother and aunts wanted her to be equipped to earn her own living by the time she reached the age of seventeen. She planned to earn money teaching, both to help pay the mortgage on Sunnybrook Farm, and to help with the education of her younger brothers and sisters back home.

Wareham was a pretty village, much larger than Riverboro, with a broad main street shaded by maples and elms. It had a pharmacy, a blacksmith's forge, a plumber, a dry-goods store, and several other shops, two churches, and a good number of boarding houses where

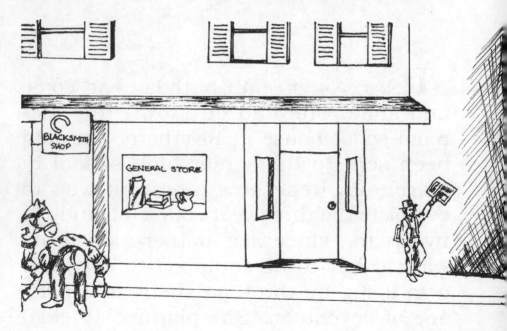

students from out of town could find lodging. The high school was the center of cultural life in the village. There was only one such establishment in the county. Boys and girls from a wide array of surrounding towns and villages gathered in Wareham to learn a profession. These students were of every type—wealthy, middle-class, and of relatively humble financial means, like Rebecca.

The school's dominance over the affairs of the town provided an opportunity for a great deal of foolish and reckless behavior. Surprisingly, students did not take advantage of their position to misbehave. There were also occasional bursts of silliness from flirtatious girls like Huldah Meserve. Her idea of fun was to have an ever-changing court of admiring boys to fetch and carry for her.

Huldah had the bad habit of bragging about the hearts she kept breaking to girls who did not have boyfriends. It did not take long for this to wreck the childhood friendship that had been established back in Riverboro among Huldah, Emma Jane, and Rebecca. Before the end of the first semester, Rebecca and Emma Jane had begun to sit at one end of the train going to and from Riverboro, while Huldah occupied the other end of the car with her court. Sometimes this company was brilliant beyond words, including a certain boy

named Monte Cristo, who often spent money on a round-trip ticket simply to accompany Huldah to Riverboro before turning around and traveling back to Wareham on the next train.

Rebecca remained more or less indifferent to boys. They were good comrades, but counted for little else. She liked studying in the same classes and at the library with them. She also enjoyed working with them on the school newspaper. But she was protected by her ideals and sense of dignity from the flirtatiousness that Huldah Meserve displayed on a daily basis.

Rebecca was principally interested in Wareham's high school for the education that was offered there. She admired one teacher above all others—Miss Maxwell, who taught English literature and composition. It was rumored that Miss Maxwell "wrote", which meant that she had published stories and essays in magazines. This height of achievement made Rebecca somewhat shy around her favorite teacher. However, she sought by every means in her power to remain, by far, the best and most interesting student in all of Miss Maxwell's classes.

After just one year of course work, Rebecca was granted a great privilege. On Fridays, from three until four-thirty in the afternoon, she was allowed to consult Miss Maxwell's collection of books, which lined two entire walls of her parlor. Every Friday for the following year, Rebecca sat in a big armchair in Miss Maxwell's parlor and read to her heart's content—poetry, biographies, novels, essays, great volumes of history and philosophy—choosing whatever she liked on any given Friday. At four-thirty, Miss Maxwell would come home from class to engage in a precious half-hour of conversation before Rebecca had to catch the train to Riverboro, where she spent every weekend helping her aunts catch up with household chores, laundry, and mending.

Late one afternoon in her senior year, Rebecca was reading *David Copperfield* when she happened to look up and see, through the window, two figures coming down the path to Miss Maxwell's house. It was Adam Ladd and Huldah Meserve. Huldah seemed to be flirting outrageously with Mr. Ladd as she picked her way through the snow in dainty black boots. Rebecca was surprised at how jealous she felt.

In the years that had passed since Rebecca fell off Mr. Ladd's porch, she had gradually come to know and like her soap sponsor. She had discovered, much to her surprise, that he was a very influential man, with controlling interests in railroads and other large businesses in the region. He was even on the board of trustees for Wareham's high school! Yet he was a man of only thirty years, not at all middle-aged, as she had thought back when she was a child of fourteen. Rebecca was astonished to

realize all at once that she could not bear to give up her share of Adam Ladd's friendship to Huldah—Huldah, so pretty and saucy, and so attentive!

Chapter 15

A Cherished Photo

Rebecca watched Huldah and Mr. Ladd part company at Miss Maxwell's gate. Huldah waved good-bye with a toss of her gorgeous red hair and continued on her way. Suddenly, the door to the parlor opened, and Mr. Ladd stood before the startled and flustered Rebecca.

"Miss Maxwell informed me that I might find Miss Rebecca Rowena Randall here reading, as is her custom on Friday afternoons," he joked with a

sweeping, gentlemanly bow in her direction. "There is a meeting of railway directors in Portland tomorrow, and I thought that I'd stop off in Wareham today to visit the school and to give my oh-so-valuable advice concerning its affairs, both educational and financial."

"I still can't get used to the fact that you're a trustee here," Rebecca said. "You seem to make light of the power you have. But I know that you're very interested in the school and that you do give very sound advice concerning its affairs—both educational and financial."

"You are remarkably wise and intelligent for your seventeen years," Mr. Ladd said as he settled into a chair by the fire. "The fact is, I accepted the trusteeship in memory of my mother, whose happiest years were spent here. She died when I was eight. The school might have existed for twenty or twenty-five years at that point. Would you like to see a picture of her?"

Rebecca took the leather case that Mr. Ladd pulled from the breast pocket of his jacket, where he kept it close to his heart. She opened it to find an innocent, pink-and-white daisy of a face, so open and sensitive that the vision of it went straight to Rebecca's heart.

"Oh, what a sweet, lovely flower she

must have been!" Rebecca exclaimed, tears filling her eyes.

"The flower had to bear all sorts of storms," Adam Ladd said gravely. "The bitter weather of the world bowed its head and dragged it to the earth. I was only a child at the time. I could do nothing to protect her, and there was no one else to keep trouble at bay. Now I have success and money and power, everything that would have kept her alive and happy, but it is too late. All that has come to me seems so useless sometimes, since I cannot share it with her!"

Rebecca had never seen this side of Adam Ladd before. Her heart reached out to him in sympathy and understanding. "I'm so glad that you told me, and that you showed me her photo, so that I can remember her. I wish that she could have lived to see you grow up so strong and good. My mother is always sad and busy. But once, when she looked at my brother John, I heard her say, 'My children

make up for everything.' That's what your mother would have thought about you—I'm sure of it."

"You are such a comfort to me, Rebecca," Adam said as he rose from his chair to leave. "What am I going to do when you leave this place, when you've become a schoolteacher in stylish suits in some faraway place? You'll have no time for me anymore. Please don't give me up until you have to!"

"Oh, I won't, Mr. Ladd, I can promise you that. Our friendship is bound to last a long, long time," Rebecca replied as she shook Adam's hand good-bye.

"By the way," Adam said as he stood in the doorway, "who is that young girl with all that pretty red hair and such sophisticated manners? She escorted me down the path on my way here to see you. Do you know whom I mean?"

"It must have been Huldah Meserve," Rebecca said in a voice that she hoped sounded calm and neutral. "She is from

Riverboro and will graduate next year. She used to be a close friend of mine."

Adam looked into Rebecca's eyes, so friendly and sincere. He remembered his trip along the path with Huldah and how she had flirted with him so obviously. He then said in the most serious and genuinely affectionate way possible, "Don't pattern yourself after Huldah, Rebecca.

Clover blossoms that grow in the fields of Sunnybrook Farm may not appear beautiful next to gaudy sunflowers, but clover is sweet and wholesome, and ultimately much more beautiful."

With these words, and blushing slightly at the rather new and sudden vision he had of Rebecca as a young woman, Adam Ladd took his leave of her.

Chapter 16

Graduation Day

At last, the great day dawned for
Rebecca—the day to which she had
been looking forward for two years. It
was the first goal to be reached on her
journey toward independence as an
adult. School days were now at an end;
graduation day was at hand. It was,
even now, being heralded by the sun
rising in the eastern sky over Wareham.

Anyone who is unacquainted with life
in the country could not imagine the

importance of graduation day in a small rural community. In the matter of preparation, wealth of organizational detail, and sheer excitement, it far surpasses a wedding.

Wareham was shaken to its very center on this day of days. Mothers and fathers of all the scholars, and relatives from the remotest corners of the region, had come by train and coach and farm wagon into town. Former pupils of the high school streamed back into the

dear old village, the site of so many memorable events. Lines of buggies and wagons were parked along both sides of the shady roads leading into town, the horses swishing their tails in luxurious idleness. The streets were filled with people wearing their best clothes. The fashions included not only the latest styles, but also the well-preserved costumes of previous generations. There were all sorts and conditions of men and women—storekeepers, lawyers,

doctors, shoemakers, professors, ministers, farmers—because their children all attended high school together.

The graduates, especially the young women among them, were dressed with a completeness of detail that practically defied reason and common sense. Dotted or plain Swiss-muslin dresses were the favorite costume, but there were a few girls who perspired in white cashmere, because such dresses were thought to be useful during other seasons. Blue and pink waist ribbons fluttered in the June breeze.

Rebecca had known, early on, that her mother would be too burdened with farmwork to attend the ceremony. She had also realized that her aunts could not afford to buy material for a special graduation dress. So she and Emma Jane had explored Emma Jane's attic, where they found a great deal of white butter muslin, often called cheesecloth. It was commonly used to strain preserves

during jelly-making season. They decided that the material, although not usually employed for making dresses, would just have to do in a pinch.

Emma Jane could have afforded dotted Swiss muslin instead, but she decided to follow her friend in cheesecloth as she had stood by her through other trials and tribulations. The stitches that went into pleating and tucking the inexpensive material, worth only three or four pennies per yard, made the dresses altogether lovely. Rebecca and Emma Jane could have given sewing lessons to their classmates who were dressed in silks and other expensive materials.

The class of which Rebecca was president was not likely to follow tradition. Instead of marching two-by-two from the high school to the church, the graduating students, under Rebecca's leadership, had chosen to proceed on a sort of royal chariot. A hay cart had been decorated with green vines and bunches of daisies.

Every inch of the cart was covered in greenery. Two white horses pulled the improvised chariot. Seated on maple boughs, the girls from Rebecca's graduating class waved to the assembled crowds. The boys marched behind the vehicle.

Rebecca drove the cart, seated on a greenery-covered bench that looked somewhat like a throne for a fairy princess. Tall and slender, her dark hair braided into a crown on her head, the fire of youthful joy in her face, Rebecca seemed like a young muse or wood nymph. The flowery hay cart, with its freight of blooming girlhood, looked like an allegorical painting depicting "The Morning of Life".

The people gathered for the ceremony applauded and cheered as the chariot of graduates drove past. Proud parents and friends did not stop applauding and cheering during the actual ceremony, either, although the principal tried to

keep his mood serious to match the ostensible gravity of the occasion.

During the ceremony, Rebecca was awarded a prize of fifty dollars for an essay she had written, entitled "The Rose of Joy". At the announcement of the prize, Jeremiah Cobb jumped up and cheered until he was hoarse. Mrs. Cobb was glad that they were seated near the back of the church, because her husband made a spectacle

of himself in his enthusiasm for Rebecca's fine achievement.

When the diplomas were presented, all students came forward in turn to claim their roll of parchment from the principal, acknowledging him with a bow that had been the subject of anxious thought and practice for weeks. Rounds of applause greeted each graduate at this thrilling moment. Mr. Cobb's behavior when Rebeccca came

forward became even more flamboyant. His clapping and stomping made for a week's worth of gossip in both Wareham and Riverboro. Old Mrs. Webb claimed that, during two hours of his antics, Jeremiah Cobb had simply worn out her pew—carpet, cushions, and woodwork—worn it out more than she had by sitting in it for forty years!

After the ceremony, Mr. Cobb and Mr. Ladd encountered one another during the reception. They had a lively conversation about Rebecca, both of them bursting with love and pride.

"I suppose up in Boston, girls as pretty and as accomplished as Rebecca are as thick as blackberries on the bush?" asked Mr. Cobb, beaming and nodding in the direction where Rebecca was standing with Emma Jane, talking to Mrs. Cobb.

"There may well be such young ladies," smiled Mr. Ladd, noting the old man's mood, "but I don't happen to know of any

who compare more favorably."

"My eyesight's so poor," Mr. Cobb confessed. "That's probably why she looked to me to be the most beautiful girl up on that platform."

"There's no failure in my eyes," Mr. Ladd replied. "That's just how she looked to me. You manage to see quite well, in fact—I wouldn't go to the eye doctor just yet."

"What did you think of her voice when they all sang those choruses? Anything special about it? I'm no judge of these matters," admitted Mr. Cobb.

"Her voice made the others sound poor and thin by comparison, I thought," was Adam Ladd's reply.

"Well, I'm glad to hear your opinion, you being a well-traveled young man and all that," said Mr. Cobb. "Mrs. Cobb says that I'm foolish about Rebecca and have been since the first day I drove her to Riverboro. My wife scolds me for spoiling her, but she spoils her as much as I do. Mercy! It just makes me sick at heart, thinking of all those parents of those other graduates traveling all this way to see their children graduate, and then having to compare them with Rebecca once they got here. Well, it sure was nice talking to you, Mr. Ladd. Come visit us in Riverboro some time soon."

"I'll plan on it at the first opportunity, Mr. Cobb!" Adam said heartily as he shook the hand of Rebecca's other admirer.

As Mr. Cobb walked away, Adam turned and once again admired Rebecca. He remembered their first meeting when she was fourteen, and marveled at how much she had grown. The smart and sassy girl who had once sold him soap was now a sophisticated young woman, ready to take on the world with zest, enthusiasm, and a kind heart.

Chapter 17

Looking Toward
the Future

Mrs. Cobb had come to the graduation ceremony with a troubling piece of
news in her heart. She waited until the
end of the celebration to break the news
to Rebecca.

"I don't quite know how to tell you
this, my sweet Rebecca. I wanted this
day to be perfect for you. We're all so
very proud of your accomplishments, of
the person you have made of yourself. I
wanted you to have all the happiness

and fun you so richly deserve today," Mrs. Cobb began, struggling mightily with what she had to tell Rebecca.

"What's the matter? It's about my aunts, isn't it? Are they ill? I haven't yet seen them today!" Rebecca was begining to panic.

"Your Aunt Miranda had a bad stroke this morning when she and Jane were getting ready to drive over to Wareham for your ceremony," said Mrs. Cobb. "Jane said that we weren't to let you know anything about it until the exercises were all over. She made me promise to make it seem like a normal day, a day of celebration. I'm sorry I kept it a secret from you, but I had to do it. Jane insisted that we do it this way."

"Let me get my things, and I'll go home with you this instant!" Rebecca exclaimed. "I just have to run and tell Miss Maxwell. She and I were supposed to visit the school in Edgewood, where I'm scheduled to begin teaching this fall.

Poor Aunt Miranda! And I have been so happy today, so unthinkingly happy!"

"There's no harm in being happy, love. That's the way Jane wanted you to feel today. Emma Jane can help you pack your trunk and get your room in order before we leave. Jeremiah will drive you home in the coach, just like old times."

When Rebecca arrived home, it was after dark. The door to Miranda's sick-room was open. Rebecca entered quietly, clutching the daisies she had brought home as a gift. Miranda's pale, sharp face looked very tired on the pillow. Her body was pitifully still under the blankets of her bed.

"Come in," Miranda said, turning her eyes on her niece. "Don't mess up the bed with those flowers, now."

"Certainly not, Aunt Miranda! They're going to fit nicely in this glass pitcher," said Rebecca, turning to the washstand as she tried to control her voice and stop the tears that had sprung to her eyes.

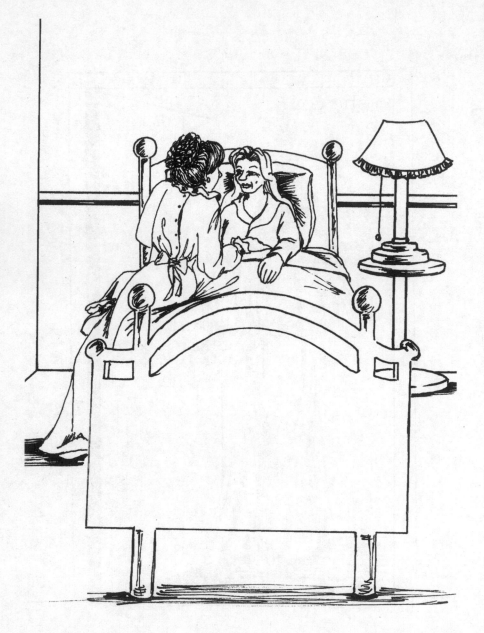

"Let me look at you. Come closer! What dress are you wearing?" demanded the invalid, trying to move her stiffened body so she could see better.

"My graduation dress, darling aunt," Rebecca replied softly. She sat down by the bedside and timidly touched her aunt's hand. Her heart swelled with tenderness at the sight of Miranda's drawn, pain-filled face.

"I am dreadfully ashamed to have you graduate in cheesecloth, Rebecca, but we just couldn't afford to spend money on new dress material. I'll try to make it up to you someday. I'm afraid you must have been the laughingstock of the whole high school!"

"It's all right, Aunt Miranda. Don't trouble yourself about me at all. Ever so many people said that our dresses were the very prettiest. They looked just like they were made of soft lace. I don't want you to worry about anything at all. Here I am, all grown up and graduated—number three in a class of twenty-two, Aunt Miranda! I've had a good teaching position offered to me already, at the Edgewood School. I'll be close enough to stay here nights and on the weekends, to help you and Aunt Jane."

There was a long pause, as Miranda struggled with her fatigue. "You listen to me," she said when she had the strength. "You do what you need to do for yourself and for your family. Your mother comes first, regardless of my sickness. I'd like to live long enough to know that you've paid off that mortgage on the farm, but I guess I won't last that long. Now, go and get your Aunt Jane. I need to speak to her a minute."

Here Miranda ceased speaking abruptly, having talked more than she knew was wise. Rebecca kissed Miranda on the forehead, whispered that she loved her, and crept from the room. By the time Jane entered, Miranda had fallen asleep. Jane waited until the next

day, when she brought toast and tea to the sickroom, to remind her elder sister about the summons.

"I need to settle the future, before I go, Jane," Miranda began firmly to speak her mind. "There are things I need to talk over with you. We need to get everything worked out now, rather than later. So don't interrupt, and don't tell me I've got time, yet, because I'm not sure I do. When I'm dead and buried, I want you to bring Aurelia and the children down here to the brick house. I've put the house in Rebecca's name in my will, so she'll inherit it. I know that she'll want you to stay here, even once she's married. Try to get Aurelia to sell that worthless farm—it's not worth the interest on the mortgage that she's been paying all these years."

"I think there's a good possibility that Adam Ladd plans to buy that land for

the new railroad he's building," Jane said gently. "He's willing to pay six thousand dollars for it—much more than it's worth. That'll give all of us a good income. So don't you fret about money anymore, Miranda. We'll all be all right."

"Well, I will admit that that piece of news takes a load off my mind. That Adam Ladd is a really nice fellow, if you ask me. A fool to sink that kind of money into that Sunnybrook Farm of

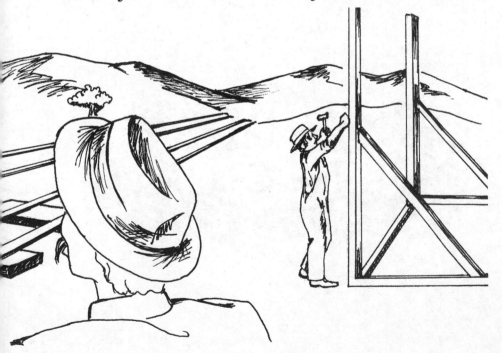

Rebecca's, but a thoughtful, generous soul all the same. Now, if you'll draw the curtains, I think I'll try to nap a little while." Miranda closed her eyes, a smile playing on her lips for the first time in weeks. She could seek peace, now that her affairs were settled for the good of all, especially for her niece Rebecca, of whom she had grown rather fond over the years they had spent together.

The End

ABOUT THE AUTHOR

Kate Douglas Wiggin was born in Philadelphia, Pennsylvania, in 1856. At age 17, she moved to California to become an educator. Once there, she founded her own kindergarten and opened a training school for teachers. Wiggin continued to teach at the school that she founded until the late 1880s.

In 1903, Wiggin published *Rebecca of Sunnybrook Farm.* It became an instant classic, and today it remains her most popular work. Other books by Wiggin include *The New Chronicles of Rebecca* (a follow-up to *Rebecca of Sunnybrook Farm*) and such lesser-known titles as *The Village Watch Tower* and *The Birds' Christmas Carol.* Wiggin died in 1923.

Treasury of Illustrated Classics ™

Adventures of Huckleberry Finn
The Adventures of Robin Hood
The Adventures of Sherlock Holmes
The Adventures of Tom Sawyer
Alice in Wonderland
Anne of Green Gables
Black Beauty
The Call of the Wild
Gulliver's Travels
Heidi
Jane Eyre
The Legend of Sleepy Hollow
& Rip Van Winkle
A Little Princess
Little Women
Moby Dick
Oliver Twist
Peter Pan
Rebecca of Sunnybrook Farm
Robinson Crusoe
The Secret Garden
Swiss Family Robinson
Treasure Island
20,000 Leagues Under the Sea
The Wizard of Oz